# Dani Binns
## Fix-it er

Written by Lisa Rajan

Illustrated by Alessia Trunfio

**Collins**

# Chapter 1

Dani Binns sat by the old toy box in the spare bedroom. She lifted the lid, smiling at her big sister Tara. Every time she took something from the box, she was sent off on an adventure to try out a new job.

As she picked out a ball of wool, her hand began to tingle. The tingling spread up her arm and around her whole body.

*Maybe I'll be knitting clothes?* she thought, as she felt herself spinning away through space and time …

# Chapter 2

When the spinning stopped, Dani found herself on a farm. She could hear sheep bleating, chickens clucking and a horse neighing. *It's so noisy*, she thought.

"Hello, I'm Asha and this is Tai," said a girl carrying a bale of hay. "We're farmers and it's feeding time. Wellies on! We'll start with the sheep."

"Hey!" called Tai, opening the gate to the sheep's field. "How did *she* get in here?"

Hannah the horse was trotting around the field, bothering the sheep. They scurried in all directions to get away.

Dani noticed that the gate between this field and the next was open. The string that tied the gate shut had been chewed through.

"Are any of the sheep missing?" asked Tai.

"It's hard to count them when they're running around," replied Asha.

Asha tried to count the sheep and lambs. Tai caught Hannah's halter and led her back to her own field. She snorted and shook her mane.

"We need to tie that gate shut, but how?" asked Tai, offering Hannah an apple.

"My wool!" remembered Dani, unwinding the ball.

Hannah stamped her hoof and neighed crossly.

Dani looked up and pointed. "Ahh … I think I know why she left her field!"

# Chapter 3

Chickens!

They were all in a flap and must have frightened the horse out of her own field.

"How did *they* get in here?" said Tai.

Dani looked at the fence between Hannah's field and the chicken yard. Two of the mossy green fence posts had been pushed apart to make a gap.

*Could chickens do that?* wondered Dani. *And why would they want to leave their yard?*

Tai ushered the squawking chickens back into their yard.

Dani stepped between the hoofprints in the mud to fix the fence with her wool.

"They won't go near their henhouse," said Tai, trying to tempt the chickens with some corn.

12

"Dani!" shouted Asha from the quad bike. "Tell Tai that one of the ewes is missing!"

Dani eyed the henhouse. *Hmmm ... I wonder ...*

She opened the henhouse door and peered inside.

# Chapter 4

*Baaaaaa!*

There she was – the missing ewe! And there was something else snuggled next to her mossy, muddy fleece – a newborn lamb!

"Asha! Tai!" called Dani, beckoning them over.

"It's not *one* sheep you are missing … it's two. Look!" beamed Dani.

Asha checked the mother and her baby to make sure both were OK.

"How did you know to look in here?" Asha asked Dani.

15

"The ewe left a trail of clues –" said Dani, "wool on the fence, muddy hoofprints … and this!" Dani gently plucked a frayed piece of green string from the sheep's mossy fleece.

"I think she wanted to find a quiet place to have her lamb, so she chewed through the string, pushed the gate open, squeezed through the mossy fence and splashed through the mud to get to the henhouse," explained Dani.

"Let's leave her in peace and finish fixing those fences," smiled Asha.

"Do you want the rest of the wool?" said Dani, handing Asha the ball.

"It was *you* who tied up the loose ends, not your wool," grinned Asha. "You're great at understanding and looking after animals. You keep the wool, as a souvenir of your farmyard fun!"

As Dani took the wool from Asha, she felt a tingle in her hand. Then her arm. Then her whole body started spinning and tumbling, away from the farm …

# Chapter 5

When the spinning stopped, Dani found herself back in the spare bedroom.

"That ball of wool has shrunk," remarked Tara, as Dani put it back in the toy box.

"I was a farmer with things to fix and some woolly problems to solve –" explained Dani, "crazy chickens, a headstrong horse and a stray sheep. But I knitted all the clues together!"

"It sounds like the toy box gave you more than you *baaaaar*gained for!" laughed Tara.

# Jobs to do on the farm

23

# Ideas for reading

Written by Clare Dowdall, PhD
*Lecturer and Primary Literacy Consultant*

**Reading objectives:**
- discuss the sequence of events in books and how items of information are related
- discuss and clarify the meanings of words, linking new meanings to known vocabulary
- answer and ask questions
- predict what might happen on the basis of what has been read so far

**Spoken language objectives:**
- use relevant strategies to build their vocabulary
- use spoken language to develop understanding through speculating, hypothesising, imagining and exploring ideas

**Curriculum links:** PSHE: Citizenship; How to keep animals safe; What farmers do

**Interest words:** bleating, neighing, squawking, scurried, ushered

**Resources:** paper, paint and pencils for drawing and painting; ICT for research

## Build a context for reading
- Look at the front cover image and read the title *Fix-it Farmer*. Ask children about any experiences that they have visiting farms.
- Discuss what Dani might be holding and doing in the picture.
- Read the blurb together. Check that children understand the phrase *in a flap*. Ask why this is a good choice of language for describing an upset on the farm. Notice the alliteration: *soothe the sheep …*

## Understand and apply reading strategies
- Read pp2–5 with the group. Model reading with expression, then encourage children to read aloud, using voices and expression to bring the characters to life.
- Look at the italicised text on p3. Ask children to suggest why these words are in italics. Explain that these are Dani's thoughts, not speech.